Blue-Footed Booby:
Bird of the Galápagos

Adapted by Nicholas Millhouse
From a story by Margret Bowman

With
paintings by Margret Bowman

Walker and Company
New York, New York

First published in the United States of America
in 1986 by the Walker Publishing Company, Inc.

Published simultaneously in Canada by John Wiley & Sons
Canada, Limited, Rexdale, Ontario.

Library of Congress Cataloging-in-Publication Data

Millhouse, Nicholas.
   Blue-Footed Booby : bird of the Galapagos.
   1. Blue-footed booby—Juvenile literature. 2. Birds—Galapagos
Islands—Juvenile literature. I. Bowman, Margret. II. Title.
QL696.P48M55   1986   598.4'3   85-27617
ISBN 0-8027-6628-5
ISBN 0-8027-6629-3 (lib. bdg.)

Printed in Hong Kong by South China Printing Co.

10 9 8 7 6 5 4 3 2 1
Text Design by Laurie McBarnette

Halfway between the North and South Poles lie several small islands called the Galápagos. They are surrounded by the Pacific Ocean.

On one of these islands, a blue-footed seabird watched over its newly hatched chick named Booby.

Booby was not alone on the hot, dusty floor of the ancient volcano. He was surrounded by many noisy parents who were protecting their young from the midday sun. There were one or two chicks in most of the nests; a few nests even had three.

The deep blue sky was alive with soaring mother and father blue-footed boobies. They were taking turns searching for food. Birds constantly disappeared and reappeared over the rim of the crater. One parent always stayed at the nest to guard the chicks.

Out of the sky swooped Booby's father. Smaller and quicker than Booby's mother, he could dive safely into shallow water. He found food near the shore, close to the nest.

Booby gently prodded his father's throat and cried, "Aark, aark." When his father opened his beak wide, young Booby thrust his head deep into his father's gullet. There he found several fresh silver anchovies. Booby quickly gulped down his meal.

Booby's stomach was full. He nestled against the
soft feathers of his mother's breast and, even though his
neighbors were noisy and restless, went to sleep.

All around him hundreds of birds were clicking their beaks, stretching their wings, lifting their bright blue feet in the air, and pointing their beaks to the sky. Fathers whistled and mothers quacked. Everywhere there was movement and excitement.

Day by day, Booby grew larger and stronger, and his stiff brown wing feathers pushed through the white down.

When Booby was three months old, he was almost as big as his father. For many days, Booby flapped his wings and practiced flying. He landed on his belly. He fell on his head. He bumped into neighbors. Gradually he learned what not to do.

One day he flew so high that he cleared the rim of the crater. Now he was gliding over the immense blue sea. Soon he was rising and falling in gusts of wind. Large waves rolled onto the rocky shore. He nearly crashed into the snorting sea iguanas, who were sunning themselves on the black lava. They looked like small dinosaurs. Red Sally Lightfoot crabs with their light-blue undersides scurried over everything.

For the first time Booby saw live fishes in the sea. When he was older, he would be able dive into the water and catch some.

Booby landed on a lava ledge and watched the iguanas disappear below the surface of the ocean to chew on red and green seaweeds. On land, the male iguanas bobbed their heads while the females remained as still as the rocks on which they were standing. When frightened, they would run away, scraping their claws on the rocks.

A scaly iguana stood near Booby. Its powerful claws clutched the tiny holes of the volcanic rock. The iguana bobbed its head and snorted, sending a spray of salt water at Booby. Booby raised his wings, but the iguana was not frightened and scampered away to sun himself on a rock nearby.

Not far from shore, a giant tortoise, or galápago,
lumbered by Booby. Its small head was held high at the
end of a very long neck that was covered with wrinkled
skin. Its legs were round and thick.

A short distance away, another tortoise was making a shallow nest in the ground by stamping with her hind feet. She wet the nest with her urine. This turned the dry soil to mud. Then, one by one, six eggs plopped into the nest. When they were laid, the tortoise scraped mud over the eggs with the flat bottom of her shell. Then she moved away.

Without looking behind her, the tortoise began to plod back to the cooler hills, leaving the eggs to hatch in the sun-warmed soil.

Most of the trees near the shore were Opuntia cactus. They were very tall. Their trunks were thick and stiff and covered with orange bark. Their stems were green pads covered with long prickly spines. Each pad looked like a flat pincushion. Sometimes yellow flowers appeared from stubby buds on the edges of the pads.

The tortoise slowly stumbled and bulldozed its way among the cactus trees. A vermilion flycatcher often perched on the tortoise's shell and darted back and forth looking for insects.

The tortoise bumped into the trunk of a cactus tree, and a spiny green pad fell to the ground with a thud. The tortoise stretched out its neck and bit off a juicy piece. It even gulped down the spines!

Not far away was another cactus-eater. This round-tailed land iguana was munching a cactus pad and its yellow flowers. Before biting into the pad, the iguana scraped away most of the spines with his foot. All the cactus food quickly disappeared behind a row of tiny teeth in the huge jaws.

Booby returned to the crater, and both his parents
fed him several fish. As each day passed, he became
stronger. He began to dive for anchovies and catch
enough to feed himself. Now, he flew more often and to
more distant places.

One day, as Booby flew over one of the islands,
he saw grey and black finches building nests between

the prickly pads of the cactus. They had woven dried grass and dead twigs into a small hollow ball. It had a hole at one side that was used as a doorway. Three wide-open beaks were waiting for food from the mother and father finches.

On the rotten limb of a nearby tree, another kind of finch was digging for food. In its beak, it held a cactus spine that was used as a tool. The bird poked the spine into a hole, and before long a large caterpillar wriggled out trying to escape. The finch quickly gobbled it up and then continued to dig for more food.

There was a sudden rush of hot wind. Booby twisted and turned on his strong wings as he circled high above the island.

Below him, the damp ground of the highlands was covered with mosses, ferns, and grasses. Plants called lichens draped the crooked trunks and branches of trees. The air was still as night fell. The only sounds were those of bats squeaking as they fluttered about. Large-eyed owls swooped among the shadows.

Booby went back to the crater for the night.

Early the next morning, Booby flew over a shallow pond where some tortoises had spent the night. Only their heads and the tops of their shells stuck out of the water. Here, in the cool, moist uplands, they could spend much of their time grazing on green plants.

Booby landed on a flat rock at the edge of the water. Strange birds surrounded him. They were flightless cormorants. With their stunted wings, they could not fly but were expert at diving and at catching fish and octopus with their long, narrow beaks. They propelled themselves with large webbed feet.

Nearby, a Galápagos penguin plunged feet first into the sea. It used its wings like flippers, to "fly" underwater to catch fish.

Cormorants and penguins gather where the sea is cold and there are plenty of anchovies and flying fish.

Booby spent some time diving and fishing and then flew on.

In the sea about the Galápagos Islands, Booby's favorite food was flying fish. They were plentiful but not always easy to catch. With practice, Booby became more skilled at diving and swimming underwater. The few flying fish that escaped him came out of the water and glided on their winglike fins.

Booby was now on his own and did not go back to the crater until it was time for him to help raise his own chick.

Afterword

The South American country of Ecuador is just slightly larger than California. Its population is just less than that of New York City's (10,000,000). You can fly there in under seven hours and enjoy the eternal spring-like weather of its capital, Quito.

Six hundred miles west, into the Pacific Ocean, there are several small islands. The equator passes through them. These are the mysterious, volcanic Galápagos Islands where this story takes place.

Just imagine. You can take a small boat along with a few friends and sail around these islands. In the daytime, you can wade ashore from a panga (small boat) and walk amongst thousands of busy, noisy animals. They hardly notice you.

At night you sleep on your small boat in one of the many bays. The boat gently bobs and rocks under millions of stars, a celestial foliage. Underneath, in the clear water, sea lions weave a trail of iridescent plankton as they play. This is true peace, real adventure.

One of the strangest birds on the islands is the blue-footed booby. Its scientific name is Sula nebouxii. It is the subject of our story.

Nicholas Millhouse